The treasure house

Charlie lived in a cottage with
his dog, Rags, and his cat, Marmalade.
Behind the cottage, Charlie had
a garden. It was full of flowers,
fruit trees and vegetables.

In autumn, leaves fell from the fruit trees.
They lay on the cottage and the garden.

In winter, snow sometimes
covered the cottage.

In spring, the garden was
full of flowers.

In summer, Charlie sat
in his garden in the warm sun.
Charlie's garden was always tidy.

The inside of Charlie's cottage
was never tidy.
Charlie did not throw anything away.
The cottage was a treasure house.
But Charlie could never find anything.

Andy and Lorna liked to help
their grandfather to find things.
Charlie's dog, Rags, helped too,
but Marmalade did not help.
Sometimes they all forgot
what they were looking for.

For Charlie's birthday, the
children gave him a big pen and
some sticky labels.
They told him to stick labels
on all the drawers.

Charlie emptied everything on to
the floor. He wrote labels
for all his things. He stuck
the labels on the drawers and
cupboards. Then he put
everything back.

For a time, Charlie knew
where everything was.
He looked at the labels till
he found what he wanted.
Charlie was pleased with
his labels.

The children were pleased too.
But soon they missed the fun
of looking for things.
Everything was too neat and
tidy – until Mrs Bumble came.

Charlie went out when Mrs Bumble
came to clean the cottage.

She came with brooms and mops.
She swept and she scrubbed and
she polished everything.
Charlie's labels came off.
They were all over the floor.

Mrs Bumble looked at the labels.
She knew Charlie would be upset.
So she whizzed round the rooms.
She stuck the labels back on.
But they were all
higgledy-piggledy.

Mrs Bumble picked up her brooms
and brushes and went away.
She hoped that Charlie
would not notice.

Charlie, Andy and Lorna came back.

Charlie wanted a ball of string.

He looked in the string drawer.

No string. Andy looked too.

Lorna looked in the next drawer.

No string.

They looked in the cupboard.

No string.

Andy found an old lamp shade
and a red velvet curtain.
He put the lamp shade on his head.
It made a splendid hat.
The curtain made a fine cloak.

Andy walked up and down.
He felt like a king.

Lorna found some old pegs and
some tin foil. She made some
knights in shining armour.

She marched them round and round.
Left, right, left, right.

Andy and Lorna played
all the afternoon.
Charlie smiled. He said,
"Now, what were we looking for?"

Turnip and Beetroots

Written by Monica Hughes

Illustrated by Lee Cosgrove

Mark's mum has a turnip farm.

Mark is sick of turnips.

3

Carla's dad has a
beetroot farm.

Carla is sick of roasted
beetroot and beetroot tart.

Mark and his mum load
a cart with turnips.

Carla and her dad set off for
the market.

Mark and Carla sell food to the crowd. They get lots of coins ...

... but they can not sell the
big turnip or the big beetroot.

Now Mark has the big beetroot.
Carla has the big turnip.

Yum, yum, beetroot tart for me and roast turnip for you.